What Could it Be?

by

Carmela Castaldo

AuthorHouse™
1663 Liberty Drive
Bloomington, IN 47403
www.authorhouse.com
Phone: 833-262-8899

This book is printed on acid-free paper.

ISBN: 978-1-4343-1842-8 (sc)

Print information available on the last page.

Published by AuthorHouse

Rev. Date: 11/04/2021

authorHOUSE®

Dedicated to my grandchildren

Alexandra, Vincent, Michelle
& Christopher

What could it be?

Maybe it's------------an elephant

What could it be?

Maybe it's------------- a blue bird.

What could it be?

Maybe it's----------an owl.

What could it be?

Maybe it's- - - - - - - - - - a magical flying dog.

What could it be?

Maybe it's---------- a crocodile

What could it be?

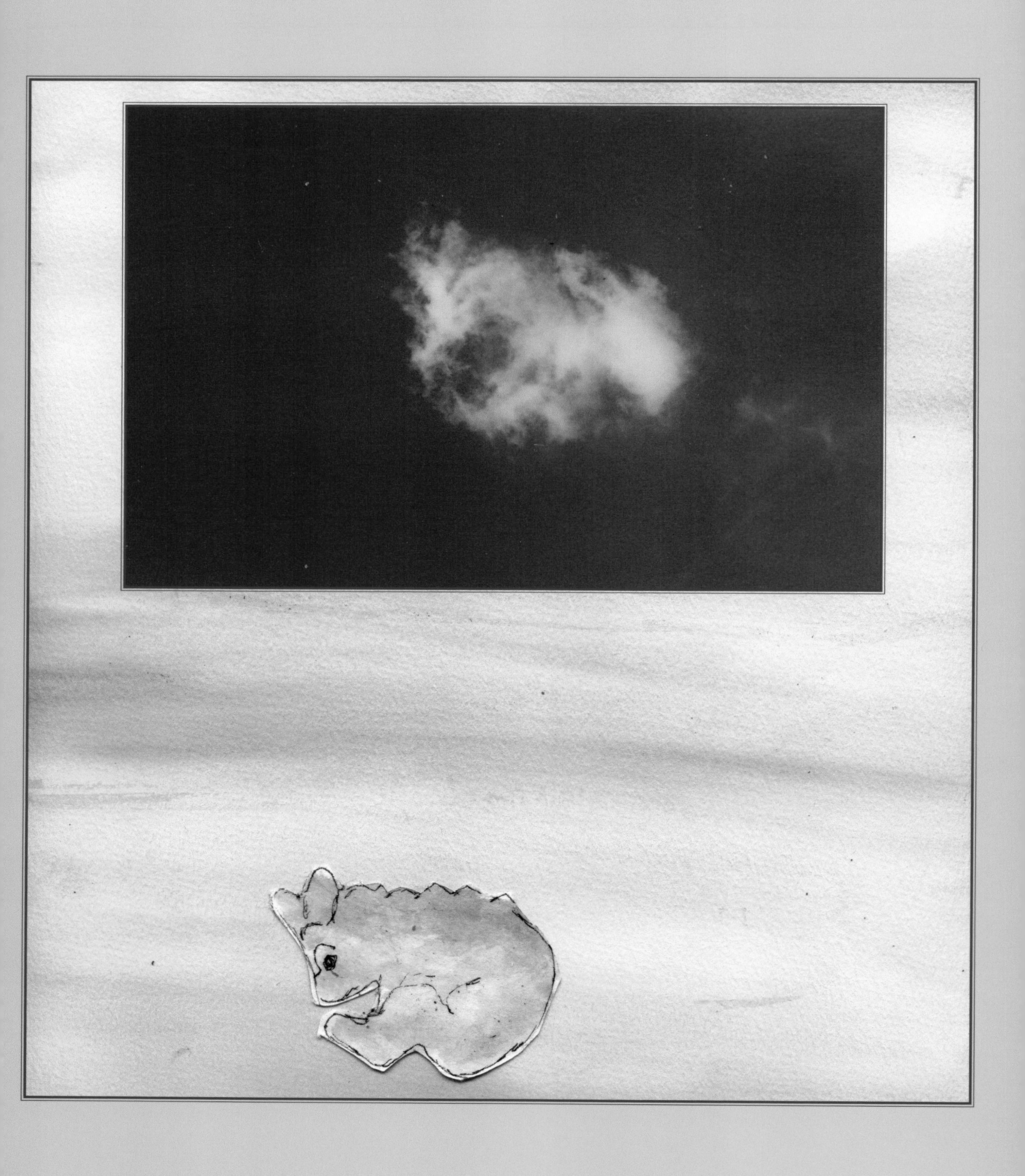

Maybe it's ---------- a baby dinosaur.

What could it be?

Maybe it's ---------- an apple tree

What could it be?

Maybe it's---------- an angel fish.

What could it be?

Maybe it's- - - - a polar bear running on ice.

What could it be?

Maybe it's----------a gray wolf.

What could it be?

Maybe it's - - - - a genie and his magic lamp.

What could it be?

Maybe it's--------- a baby flying elephant.

What could it be?

Maybe it's---------- a jumping monkey.

What could it be?

Maybe it's---------- a snail.

What could it be?

Maybe it's ---------- a Mohawk Indian.

What could it be?

Maybe it's---------Raptor (dinosaur).

What could it be?

Maybe it's---------- a funny rubber duckie.

What could it be?

Maybe it's- - - - - - - - - a funny dog begging.

What could it be?

Maybe it's- - - - - - - - - a bear.

What could it be?

Maybe it's---------a big dinosaur in a lake.

What could it be?

May it's---------- a dragon.

What could it be?

Maybe it's ------ a big mouth rainbow fish.

What could it be?

Maybe it's---------- a peacock.

Printed in the United States
by Baker & Taylor Publisher Services